W9-CFB-001

THE SNATCHABOOK

STORY BY
HELEN DOCHERTY

ILLUSTRATED BY
THOMAS DOCHERTY

sourcebooks
jabberwocky

One dark, dark night in Burrow Down,
a rabbit named Eliza Brown
found a book and settled down…

when a Snatchabook
flew into town.

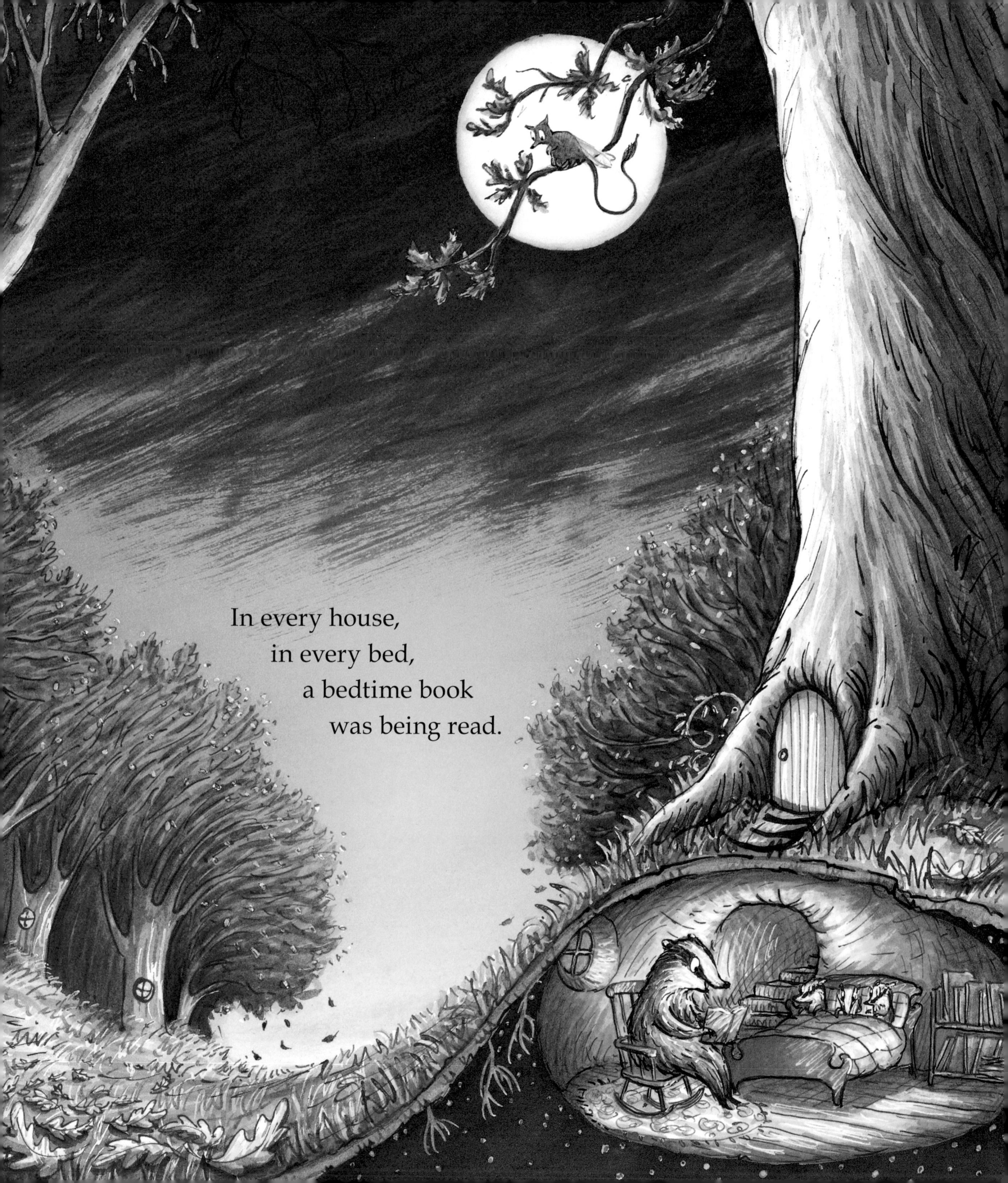

In every house,
in every bed,
a bedtime book
was being read.

Tales of dragons, spitting flames;
Witches playing spooky games;

Pirates on the seven seas;

Princesses trying to sleep on peas.

And every child in every bed,
listened hard to each word said.

Eliza Brown, at Number Three,
was reading quite contentedly.

Her curtains opened, just a chink.
She barely had a chance to blink.
Her storybook just disappeared!

Eliza found that very weird.

The little owls, on Mommy's lap,
were quite surprised to hear a tap
against their bedroom window glass.
Tap, tap! The noise came really fast.
Before they'd even looked around,
the book was gone—without a sound.

The wind blew wild across the sky.
The smallest squirrel heard a cry.
"What's that?" she whispered to her dad.

But then—*and this was really bad*—
before they'd had a chance to look,
she'd lost her very favorite book.

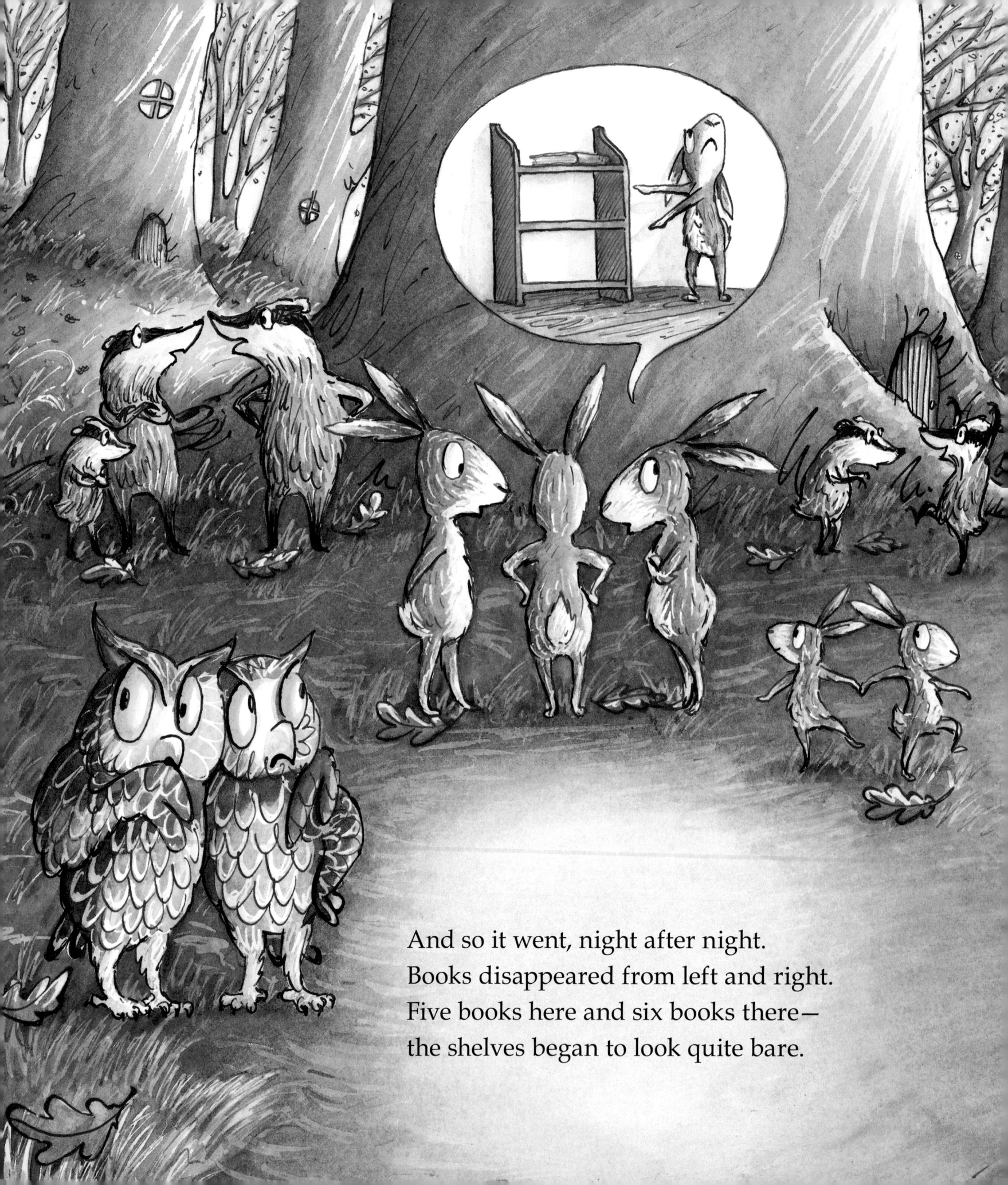

And so it went, night after night.
Books disappeared from left and right.
Five books here and six books there—
the shelves began to look quite bare.

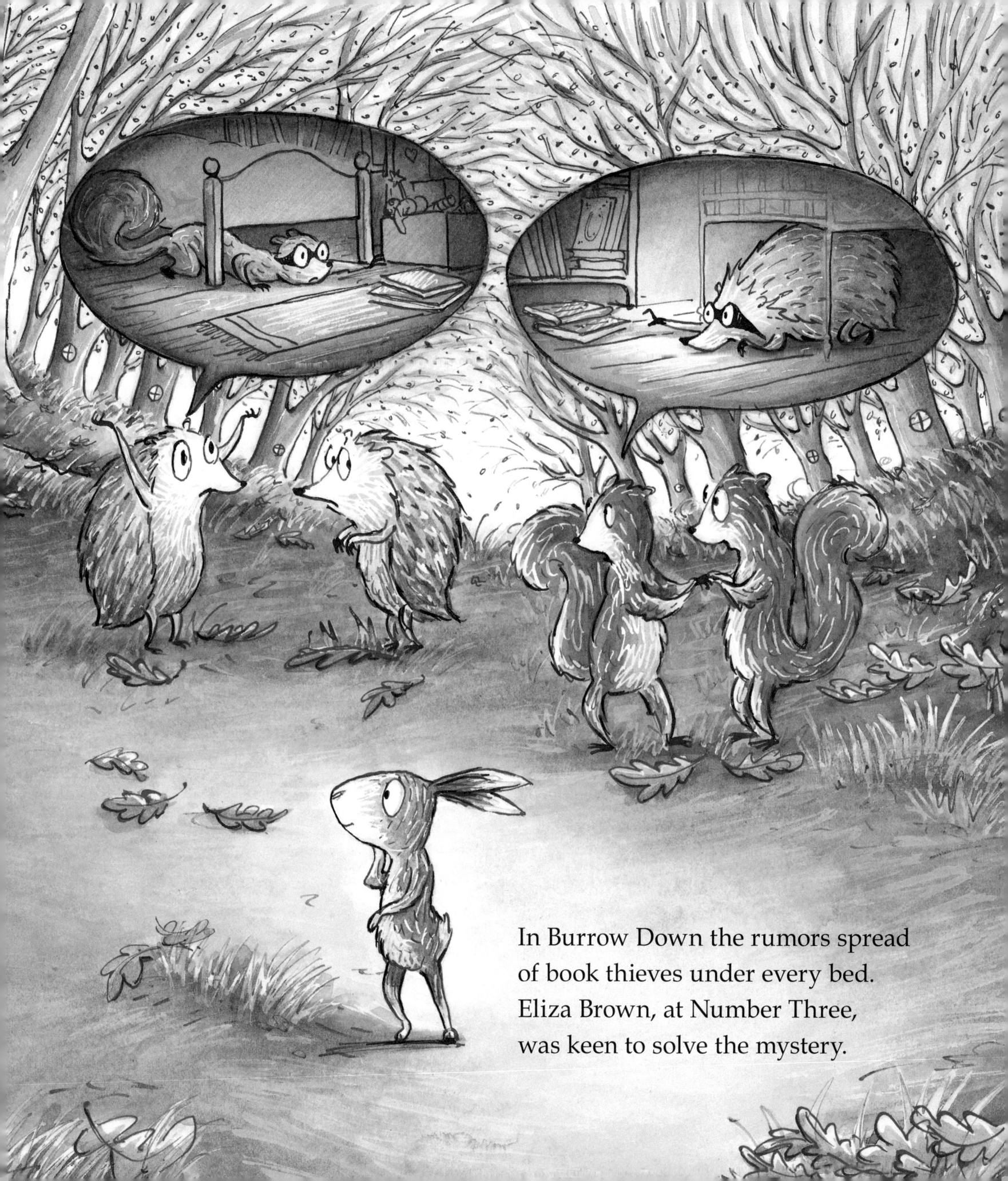

In Burrow Down the rumors spread
of book thieves under every bed.
Eliza Brown, at Number Three,
was keen to solve the mystery.

She planned one night to lie in wait
and use a pile of books as bait.

Long hours passed without a peep
(she'd nearly fallen fast asleep)

when, **suddenly**, Eliza heard
a flap of wings:
a bat?
A bird?

Eliza saw a shadow loom,
enormous—right across her room.
What kind of monster could it be?
Eliza thought: You don't scare me!

And yet, her heart was beating fast—
she'd have to face the thief at last…

She threw the window open wide
and shouted to the Thing outside:
"Stop stealing
all our books,
right now!
Just give them back,
I don't care how!"

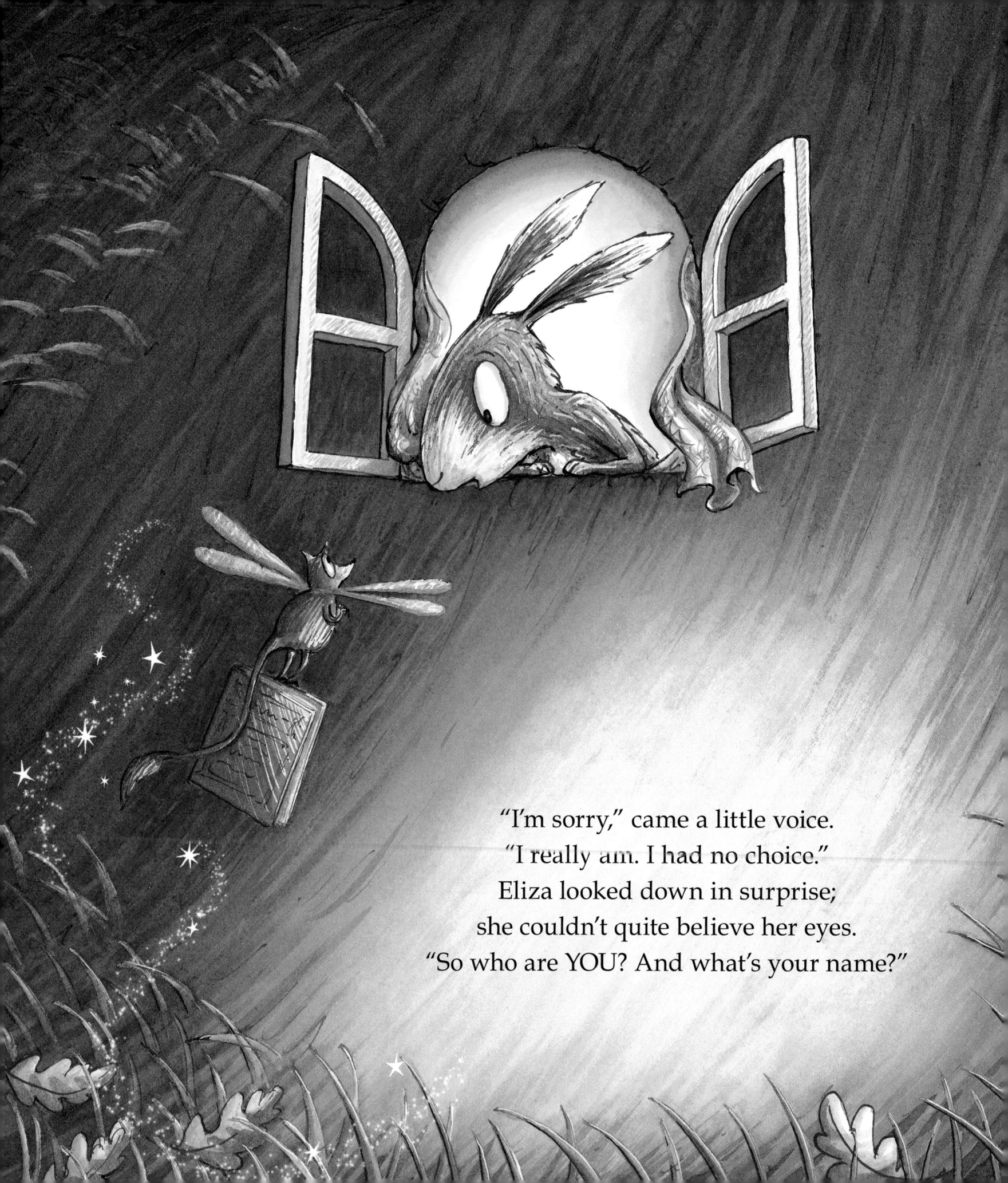

"I'm sorry," came a little voice.
"I really am. I had no choice."
Eliza looked down in surprise;
she couldn't quite believe her eyes.
"So who are YOU? And what's your name?"

The creature hung its head in shame.
He mumbled, with a mournful look,
"I'm just a little Snatchabook."

Eliza nodded solemnly.
She sat the creature on her knee.
"You can't just come and help yourself
to every book on every shelf!"

A tear rolled from the creature's eye,
and softly he began to cry.
"I know it's wrong, but can't you see—
I've got no one to read to me!"

Eliza sighed. He looked so sad.
If he just had a mom or dad
to read him stories every night—
well, then he might behave all right!

That very night,
they hatched a plan.

And so, the Snatchabook began…

…to give back all the books he'd picked.

(Eliza Brown was very strict.)

Then, trying hard to prove himself,

he stacked them neatly

on each shelf.

And when he'd made his full amends,
Eliza called on all her friends,
and told them how he'd worked all night
to turn a wrong into a right.

And now each night in Burrow Down,
as darkness falls upon the town,
in every house, in every bed,
a bedtime book is being read.

And if you take a closer look
you might just see the Snatchabook,
perched happily on someone's bed…
listening hard to each word said.

For our parents, who always read to us,
and for our daughters, Lucia and Bethan.

Copyright © 2013, 2021 by Helen Docherty and Thomas Docherty
Cover and internal design © 2013, 2021 by Sourcebooks
Text © Helen Docherty
Illustrations © Thomas Docherty

Sourcebooks and the colophon are registered trademarks of Sourcebooks.

All rights reserved. No part of this book may be reproduced in any form or by any electronic or mechanical means including information storage and retrieval systems—except in the case of brief quotations embodied in critical articles or reviews—without permission in writing from its publisher, Sourcebooks.

The characters and events portrayed in this book are fictitious or are used fictitiously. Any similarity to real persons, living or dead, is purely coincidental and not intended by the author.

Published by Sourcebooks Jabberwocky, an imprint of Sourcebooks Kids
P.O. Box 4410, Naperville, Illinois 60567-4410
(630) 961-3900
sourcebookskids.com

Originally published in the UK by Alison Green Books, an imprint of Scholastic Ltd.

Library of Congress Cataloging-in-Publication data is on file with the publisher.

Source of Production: Wing King Tong Paper Products Co. Ltd., Shenzhen, Guangdong Province, China
Date of Production: April 2021
Run Number: 5021598

Printed and bound in China.
WKT 10 9 8 7 6 5 4 3 2 1